MW00886822

Dedicated to
budding life-long learners.
May you always relish
your ability to learn.

Bosley's First Words
Copyright © 2013 Tim Johnson
ISBN-13: 978-1492803232
ISBN-10: 1492803235

The Language Bear Bilingual Books
207-370-4298
info@theLanguageBear.com
www.theLanguageBear.com

Bosley's First Words

bǎo bǎo xué shuō huà
宝宝学说话

A dual language book in Mandarin Chinese and English

Zhōng yīng shuāng yǔ shū
中 英 双 语 书

Written by: Tim Johnson
Illustrated by: Ozzy Esha

This is Bosley.

He likes to play and learn.

wǒ shì bǎo bǎo。
我 是 宝宝。

Wǒ xǐ huān wán hé xué xí。
我 喜欢 玩 和 学习。

Hello!
My name is Bosley.
What's your name?

nǐ hǎo!
你 好!

wǒ de míng zì jiào bǎo bǎo.
我 的 名字 叫 宝宝.

nǐ jiào shí me míng zì ?
你 叫 什么 名字?

Bosley eats fruit.

bǎo bǎo chī shuǐ guǒ。
宝宝吃水果。

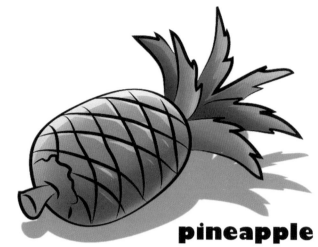

pineapple
bō luó
菠萝

orange
Jú zǐ
桔子

apple

pí ng guǒ
苹　果

banana

xiāng jiāo
香　蕉

watermelon

xī guā
西瓜

Bosley plays with toys.

bǎo bǎo wán wán jù。

宝宝玩玩具。

blocks

jī mù

积木

truck

kǎ chē

卡车

ball

qiú

球

train

huǒ chē

火车

Bosley loves his family.

bǎo bǎo ài jiā rén。
宝宝爱家人。

father
bà bà
爸爸

mother
mā mā
妈妈

brother
dì dì
弟弟

sister
mèi mèi
妹妹

grandmother
nǎi nǎi
奶奶

uncle
Shū shū
叔叔

grandfather
yé yé
爷爷

aunt
ā yí
阿姨

Bosley can count to ten.

bǎo bǎo kě yǐ shù dào shí。
宝 宝 可 以 数 到 10。

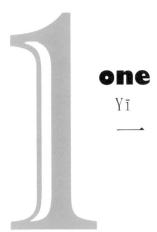
one
Yī
一

two
Èr
二

three
sān
三

four
Sì
四

five
wǔ
五

six
liù
六

seven
qī
七

eight

bā

八

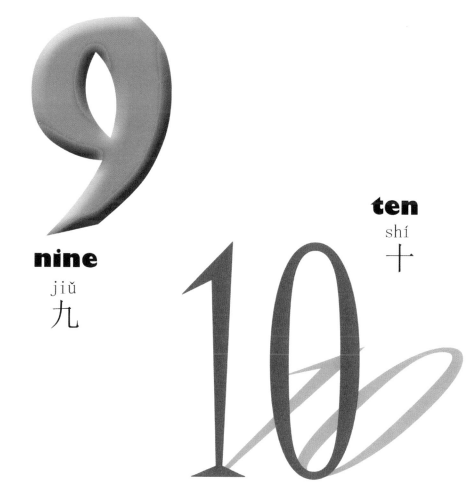

nine

jiǔ

九

ten

shí

十

Bosley likes animals.

bǎo bǎo xǐ huān dòng wù。
宝 宝 喜 欢 动 物

cat
māo
猫

dog
gǒu
狗

horse
mǎ
马

chicken
jī
鸡

pig
zhū
猪

cow
niú
牛

Bosley runs.

bǎo bǎo pǎo。
宝 宝 跑。

Bosley jumps.

bǎo bǎo tiào 。
宝 宝 跳。

Bosley plays.

bǎo bǎo wán 。

宝 宝 玩。

Bosley climbs.

bǎo bǎo pà。

宝 宝 爬。

Bosley sits.

bǎo bǎo zuò。

宝 宝 坐。

Bosley eats.
bǎo bǎo chī。
宝 宝 吃。

Bosley waves.
bǎo bǎo huī shǒu。
宝 宝 挥 手。

Bosley sleeps.
bǎo bǎo shuì jué。
宝 宝 睡 觉。

Goodnight.
wǎn ān!
晚 安!

The Adventures of Bosley Bear

Bosley Sees the World

Join Bosley Bear on his first adventure outside the cave when he discovers how big the world is and how much there is to explore. He learns about trees, birds, rocks, mountains, rivers and so much more, teaching your child as he learns.

Bosley Goes to the Beach

Bosley Bear gathers his toys and goes to the beach to make new friends and learn new words. Discovering that other animals at the beach have interesting capabilities like flying or swimming, Bosley realizes that he has something that makes him special in his own way.

Keep up with Bosley as your child grows: www.theLanguageBear.com

14644516R00015

Made in the USA
San Bernardino, CA
01 September 2014